I'M GOING
ON A GORILLA HUNT

Maurice Jones

I'M GOING ON A GORILLA HUNT

Pictures by
Charlotte Firmin

PUFFIN BOOKS

A clever hunter needs a cunning disguise

and the right equipment.

Now where would a gorilla hide?

He's not in the house.

Perhaps he's outside. I really need a better view.

But how can
I catch this
hairy monster?

How can I snare
this ugly brute?

A clever hunter tracks his prey,

and never lets him get away.

A clever hunter's never scared,
whatever happens he's prepared.

A clever hunter can be small.
Size doesn't bother him at all.

A clever hunter takes a rest

and knows what hunters like the best.

A clever hunter's brave and wise.
Nothing takes him by surprise.

Two gorillas!

Phew,
safe at last!